THE CENTRE

THE INSECURITY TRIPTYCH
THREE NOVELLAS. THREE SECURITY GUARDS.
THREE NIGHTMARES.

PROVOCATION

Anorexia nervosa survivor Madeleine Kyle embodies twenty-one years of medical intervention; a complex system of internal rules to navigate the dark tides of her fate. When she is stalked by a State Library security guard, Madeleine is pushed to the depths of her unique psyche. In a violent endgame, meaning and motive are as murky as the depths of a river in flood.

THE CENTRE

Zilla Bannich is a dark haired, thick-thighed Polish-Australian misfit on the Gold Coast. As a shopping centre security guard, Zilla is first-on-scene to an incident—a child abandoned, a mother abducted—but falls under suspicion as she clumsily taints the evidence and appears to know the child. *The Centre* explores unspoken truths of girlhood and the erotic passion of belonging, leading us to consider the freedom of love in liminal spaces.

CRAWLSPACE

In 1987, baby Marlene witnesses her father mutilated in a Port Moresby compound invasion, giving rise to a deep psychological scar and a powerful family secret. Twenty-five years later, Marlene finds her perfect match in depressed outer-suburban Brisbane. Andy is a Visa-dependent teenage American escaping his past, and a cyber-security guard who can lay his hands on your money anytime he chooses. An unplanned pregnancy gives urgency to Marlene and Andy's next scam. But who is it that watches from the crawlspace under their humble house of dreams?

THE CENTRE

INSECURITY TRIPTYCH #2

MEG VANN

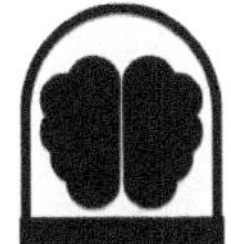

Brain Jar Press
PO Box 6687
Upper Mt Gravatt, QLD, 4122
Australia
www.BrainJarPress.com

Cover design by Peter Ball
Cover Images: Old and dusty child shoes, Zlata_Titmouse/Shutterstock

ISBN: 978-1-922479-08-2 (Print); 978-1-922479-09-9 (Ebook)

THE CENTRE

They know only the shining halls, marble slick as celebrity teeth. Glass so clean, plastic chandeliers so bright: the circus was in town every moment of every day. Each of them a gawking ticket-holder, every one of them a sideshow freak. Clothes colourful as flags, they promenade. Ridiculous shoes. Rubber thongs with sequined straps between sparkle-lacquered toes; arches flat as flipped pancakes on the glossy tiled floor.

I'm invisible to them. A grey nurse shark on a cloudy day, I slide, unnoticed, into fingerpocked anonymous doorways. Filthy corridors twine around their mirror-tiled mecca; industrial bins filled with stink and Styrofoam, faulty cable junctions snapping at the stale air.

The pink welt pangs the flesh of my palm, running from lifeline to middle finger. Guilt stippled. I rub it away with my other hand, watching it fade as I make my way into my lair; a cave filled with rolling screens and cans sticky with a residue of flat fizz. There's a soft click and whir as I switch the security cameras back on.

It's my job to keep them all safe.

I.

Tamara's thoughts roiled with cough syrup, thick and muggy. The wheels of the cheap plastic stroller jammed into a rut between the brickwork pavers of the canal walkway.

'Shitfug.' Her words slurred as she jerked the stroller back into motion. A rough, nervous hand spread on her tailbone; guiding, pressing.

Faster, faster.

'Make her be quiet, will ya.' The voice in her ear was young. Young meant inexperienced, and inexperienced meant dangerous.

'The medicine will make her sleep.'

'It's not fucking helping so far – she hasn't stopped whining since you gave it to her.'

'It'll kick in soon. It will.' She heard herself pleading, desperate to keep everyone calm: him, her, the child. She'd taken a big slug herself to keep an even keel and it was already taking effect, but down in the stroller it seemed to be working in reverse.

In a hard, high tone he'd told her no one would be around, and he was right. Despite the waterfront location, this narrow walkway was populated only by air conditioning sheds and the paspalum grass forcing its way through the gap where the pavers met the canal sea-wall. A shadow bifurcated the path, midday and midnight. He bodychecked her along the wall of the shopping centre. Twice he forced her so close that she grazed her arm on the concrete cladding, right where it had been twisted and bruised last night.

Tenderised meat.

She barely noticed until they reached the first carpark, when the blood running down her arm dripped from her pinky finger onto the bitumen. Lifting her hand in a daze, she failed to connect the shining dark spots with the pain. But he did. He grabbed her wrist and twisted; a warning growl deep in his throat. A fist of panic drove into her solar plexus as he ground the spots away with the heel of his tattered leather boot.

Bleak and pale in the searing heat, half-filled with cars under rows of grey shade tents, the carpark stretched before them. His eyes flickered from one row to the next, measuring, planning. She watched him, fighting just to stay on her feet, leaning on the handles of the pram.

Like a gunshot, a small figure burst out of the pram. The sunshade flipped up into her face before the whole thing went out from under her. Tamara's chin came down hard on the plastic bar, kneecaps cracking onto the bitumen.

'Jeeziz fuck – get the kid!'

Eyelids squeezed tight against the pain, she heard the child's cry, rich with mischief and anger. Forcing her eyes open, vision still drenched in a violent red glare. Maternal instinct guided her outstretched fingers. She tagged the girl's dress, clutching blindly, drawing her in.

'Stick her in the pram. Now!' The shaken voice was pitched so low her marrow resonated terror.

'Help me, help.' Desperation made her hoarse. 'I can't see.'

A cool shirtsleeve brushed her cheek, wrapped around her shoulders, pulled her to her feet. A small pointed elbow bumped her in the ribs and a tiny set of toes scratched her arm.

'Sh-sh-shh.'

Soothing, clucking sounds burbled underneath the child's protests until the hard click of the plastic buckle punctuated the scene. A quick gasp of pain.

Then a long-familiar voice, faint, as though directed elsewhere.

'Go.'

. . .

The radio shocked Zilla's hip with a static blast. She sluiced some water on her face, the chlorine stink of it stinging her eyes. Her left hand smeared a damp line down her coarse drill trousers as her right lifted the radio to her ear in one smooth motion.

'What's up?'

'Where the fuck are you, Zilla?' Stanno's voice rasped with fat panic. 'We gotta situation. A lost kid, looking the worse for wear. Maybe its nothing, but the kid's shirt is torn or something, so … Over in the Food Court.'

'I'm in the Ladies.' She headed for the door. 'Food Court?'

'Roger that. Near the Coffee Club.'

'On my way. What's your location?'

'South-east exit, heading west.' A dull thump and hydraulic whoosh as he shouldered open a fire exit.

'Perimeter walk?'

'Just finished.'

'Smoking will kill ya, Stanno.'

'Shut up and get moving.'

Zilla snicked him off and moved to dock her radio, then thought again. Depressed the talk button. 'Stan, how old's the kid?'

'Little kid, I think. Samaritan reported a toddler.'

'Shit.'

'Yeah.' Stanno coughed with the strain of hustling his bulk. 'Let me know if you need to call the boys.'

Zilla picked up her pace, turning right past Best and Less. Her thumping heart strained against the buttons of a too-tight shirt as she sorted through a mental checklist of first-on-scene procedures. Security Operations training only went for one week, but it covered the basics of every emergency. Zilla had spent many sleepless nights since, playing out possible scenarios in her head.

But having to deal with an actual crisis froze her ribcage solid.

She especially dreaded having to call 'the boys' in. The local coppers were surfie smart-arses who still thought a woman's place was on the beach towel. They treated her like shit. But then, that type always had.

The glass-fronted Food Court stuck out like a crooked hip towards the canal foreshore. Fixed tables left plenty of room for the prams and wheelie-walkers required by the majority of customers. Eleven o'clock on a school day, the mall wasn't busy, but a jangle of voices grew as Zilla approached. She'd never acclimatised to the way sound moved in this place, sharp and unpredictable. As she rounded the final corner, the klaxon alarm of a screaming child hit her full force. A handful of concerned shoppers formed a well-intentioned pastel wall, buzzing a unified commentary.

'Poor thing's lost her mummy.'

'Look at the state of her.'

'And crying herself sick with it, too.'

Zilla's professional resolve collapsed, her heavy boots clomping into a run towards the epicentre of the distress. An older couple stood at ground zero, with a heavily pregnant woman next to them. As one, they turned to Zilla, confusion and concern raking the clay of their tanned faces. Zilla slowed her momentum, and steadied herself, nerves taut in her throat. 'I'm with Security. Can I help? What's happened?'

The older lady shrugged her narrow shoulders, baffled at how to communicate over the din. The pregnant one simply turned aside, and as her bump rotated, a little girl came into view. The child's head was only just covered in soft, golden-brown curls. She wore a red sundress made of an exotic, embroidered fabric, and one little red shoe. Her body was rigid and bent; a runner tensed for the starting pistol. The swollen hammock of a full disposable nappy hung heavily between her legs, reaching almost to her knees. Her eyes were shut tight as a fist, her face tipped up to the glass ceiling with her lower jaw stretched open wide enough to ache. The sound she made was beyond the capacity of her small chest. Beyond human.

At the sight of that girl's face, Zilla froze.

Oh hell, did Tony find out? If that prick had wrecked their plan, she had to make sure no one found out her part in it.

'She just ran in here a few minutes ago, started screaming. She won't let us touch her,' the pregnant woman yelled, placing one clammy hand on Zilla's wrist. She leaned in further, until her warm breath filled the bowl of Zilla's sensitive ear. 'My name is Debbie. But, look. Look at the kid's legs. At the back.'

Zilla pulled away, searching the woman's round features for more: a clue, some comfort. Debbie turned towards the older couple. *Mum, Dad, step back a bit now. Let her see.*

But Zilla had already guessed what she would see. Red streaks, coin-sized purple spots; the rear of the girl's thighs looked like pepperoni pizza. All Zilla's nights of lying awake, haunted by the worst-case scenarios, manifested in those tiny legs still frozen mid-pump.

The girl's nightmare was in full swing, but Zilla's had just begun. She realized that no matter how bad this might turn out for her, it was already worse for the girl. Zilla had to protect her.

She squatted. 'Hey there, sweetie —' Procedural details swam around her head, but which procedure should she follow? Lost child, or crime scene? And either way, what the hell should she say? '— where's Mummy?'

The girl's expression didn't change, but her eyes slid

under their lashes towards the sound of Zilla's voice. She broke her relentless howl to draw in a long, jerking breath.

'Come with me, okay?' Zilla reached forward and placed two fingers on the back of the girl's wrist, an invitation to trust. Like letting a dog sniff your palm. 'I'll look after you now, okay?'

The girl jerked away, the bows of her sundress straps fluttering like nervous butterflies on her shaking shoulders. She flicked open her eyelids to reveal liquid dark iris, a thin blue margin eclipsed with pupils. 'Mummy car!' The girl threw herself at Zilla, small hands both grabbing tight and pushing her away.

'Mummycarmummycarmummycar!'

Snot and spit soaked through Zilla's shirt. Her urge to push the girl away was backed by protocol, but her heart gave a different directive. She shifted her hands slowly and brought them in front of those pinching, pummeling fists. The girl met the resistance, and dug her blade-thin nails into Zilla's palms. Zilla flinched, but held firm, slowly bringing the girl's arms down to her sides so she could reach around and hold her close. The girl gave a full body shudder, writhing from head to half-clad feet, before collapsing into Zilla's embrace. Her cries became human; heartbreaking and normal.

Zilla hugged her tightly, stroking the delicate tendrils of golden hair as she crooned to the child she had never met before. Not properly.

But she knew the girl's name. 'It's okay, Ellie. You're going to be okay.'

The hard rim of a car boot dug into the back of Tamara's thighs. She looked down on herself as through mosquito net gauze and noticed she was crying; chest juddering out of rhythm, hope leaking through closed lids.

Salted broth stung her sinus. She coughed and heaved, throwing herself forward automatically. A bucket of dirty water thrown over her shoes, and she was on the ground again.

She would tear off her own skin to escape, and toss it like a cheap coat into the warm stink of mouldy orange peel and sour vodka.

'Get up get up get up.' His bony hand in her armpit.

She braced against the side of a giant metal wall. A bin? A shed? She tried to focus. Clenched her thighs weakly, pressed one palm to the coarse gravel and raised her head.

Broken pink plastic, thrown aside in haste. Teddy bears printed on the useless sunshade.

Where was the small hand in her hand?

A dank lotus of grief dissolved her.

He tucked her in neatly, bent at the neck and knees. Lying on one side, tote bag thrown on top. Phone, cards, license — all gone, plastic-wrapped and brick-weighted on the muddy canal floor. Thin nylon carpet, the stink of glue. Every atom of heat ever generated, pressed into that airless coffin, scorching the flesh of her aching lungs.

He closed the boot clumsily, bouncing the lock twice before it clicked into place. Raced around to start the engine, cranked the aircon.

As the first cool breath through the slotted vent touched her forehead, she surrendered to death, her only freedom. She was gone, and it was forever.

Constable Roberto Farquhari squinted into the glare, pushing his sunglasses harder onto the bridge of his nose. No improvement.

Fucking Queensland fucking summer.

He passed the tea-tree swamp, grunting as fumes from the neighbouring sewage ponds seeped through his closed windows. He pulled into the double-wide entrance to the Runaway Bay Shopping Centre, glancing at the seafood restaurant that stood on its own in the North carpark. The sense-memory of garlic prawns and crisp green beans in butter snagged his attention.

Maybe after.

The tyres gave a satisfying squeal into the emergency vehicles slot. He swung his long legs out, leather runners hitting the sun-soft bitumen with an athlete's confidence. Robbie had transferred up here for special training. In a year or two, if he handled everything right, he'd be a Detective with the Criminal Investigation Bureau. He didn't know anybody on the Gold Coast, and he hadn't yet found his place in the unofficial hierarchy honeycombing the Queensland Police Service. But plain clothes, an unmarked car, and the promise of Homicide made it worth leaving Melbourne – although some days it was touch and go.

Walking through the sliding doors into a brick wall of chill, he scanned the wide marble halls. Early February, so all the kids were in school and the place was a morgue. He headed straight for the Security Control Office, tucked behind the western entrance. Through a Restricted Access door, down a narrow, dirty corridor and into a grubby room the size of a watch house cell.

Empty. Robbie's gaze perched on every surface lightly as a bird, coming to rest finally on the screen showing a paunchy security guard sitting next to a toddler in another room somewhere. He figured it was close, so stuck his head out and listened. Murmurs came from behind a nearby door. It flew open as an older guy with a big barrel belly emerged, his round face the colour of an eggplant. Despite the air con, sweat soaked through the armpits of his uniform. He didn't notice Robbie at first, still talking over his shoulder.

'They'll be here soon. You stay put and I'll go do another search for the mother. And get her to settle down, will ya? Try the lollipop again.'

Robbie took six long strides and didn't bother to stick out his hand.

'Farquhari, Runaway Bay station. In here?'

'Oh hey, you're here. It's a weird one, I gotta tell ya. All the years I been in this job, and I never –'

'Were you the first responder?' Robbie couldn't give a toss how long this loser had been sitting on his arse in a shopping centre in the middle of nowhere.

The guard squinted, his dull mind going on the defensive. Robbie rocked on his heels and waited while he slowly lifted a stubby finger and pointed into the First Aid room. Robbie blew past him and entered, the guard following, puffing and clumsy-footed.

On a low vinyl couch sat a dark-haired woman, mid-twenties. What had looked like paunch on the security video, up close reveled themselves as soft curves hugging a strong frame. Her skin was olive yet untanned, radiating a vulnerability that he recognised instantly. A survivor.

Hearing them come in, the woman lifted a pair of shadow-grey eyes from the phone in her hand, then pocketed it, turning to the little girl seated next to her. Robbie watched the woman square her shoulders, trying to be strong. He could taste the effort it cost her.

The little girl seemed comatose: tear-swollen eyes fixed on the woman's face, mouth hanging half-open and emitting a constant low keening sound. A full water bottle rested between her legs, leaning against a partly visible nappy. Robbie looked away. Seven years policing, including some pretty nasty cases, but he was still squeamish when it came to baby business.

Next to the pair was a low side-table, its surface covered with bandage wrappers, opened lolly packets, and a little red shoe. He raised his eyebrows. 'Injuries?' He took a notebook out of his back pocket, sliding a small pen out from the spiral binding. 'You were first on scene? Tell me what's happened.'

The woman snapped him a fierce look, keeping her full lips locked.

Robbie adjusted his body language. If she wanted a power struggle, she wasn't going to get one — not head on, anyway. His hands, still clutching pen and notebook, moved up and out a little in a friendly gesture of surrender. 'Plain Clothes Constable Roberto Farquhari, at your service.'

'Druzcilla Bannich. And this is Stanno. Stan Turner.'

The child twitched at the sound of the woman's voice. Stanno nodded acknowledgement.

'Okay, then. Ms. Bannich –'

'Call me Zilla.'

'Okay, Zilla. And I'm Robbie. So, were you first on scene?'

Her phone vibrated audibly from her pocket. She ignored it, keeping her gaze on him as she made a slight sideways movement with her chin. *Yes.*

'And we have a lost child?'

This time her whole head moved in confirmation.

'Is the missing adult her mother?'

Another nod. Robbie relaxed, confident he was in control of the exchange.

'Well, we assume it's her mum. No one can tell us anything much.' Zilla pointed at the closed door. 'We've been searching the centre for an hour, no sign of anything.'

'So you've spoken to some witnesses? I'll need their names, later.'

Stanno spoke up. 'No worries. I've got their names and

contact details right here.' He flipped a reporter's notebook out of his top pocket, and promptly dropped it.

'Has anyone checked the security footage?' Robbie was watching Zilla. She slid her glance to the Stanno, saying nothing.

Stanno straightened up with the notebook back in hand, harrumphing awkwardly. 'The files are — well, actually, the cameras haven't been —'

'You're kidding me.' Robbie swung around in disbelief.

'It's my job to check 'em at the start of the shift.' He stared at something on his shoe. 'Sometimes I forget.'

'Oh, Stanno, not again.' Zilla let out a long breath.

'Hang on, I was just in there. The screens were all active.' Robbie looked back and forth at the two of them, reaching for a textured knot just below the surface of their words.

'I flicked them on as soon as I noticed.' Zilla stiffened her jaw, defiant. 'The cameras are hopeless, anyway — they only cover the exits and pathways near the posh shops. They're there to stop theft, not find lost kids.'

'So do we have anything from today?'

'Only the last hour or so.'

Robbie checked his watch, then pointed at Stan, accusing. 'Log it. Do one more perimeter check, every alley, every corner, everywhere. Then sit down and log exactly what we've got on file footage.'

'Righto, on it.' Stan nodded with enthusiasm, perhaps wanting to make up for error with the surveillance, and left.

Robbie turned to Zilla, trapping air behind his lips, expelling sharply. 'Right. Do we have a name?'

She placed her hand on the girl's ankle protectively. 'This is Ellie.'

The girl's hiccups worsened, rapid little clutches of breath that cramped her face with each one. She shook Zilla's hand from her ankle, spilling the water bottle onto the floor with a slap. They all ignored it.

'And the mother?'

'I believe it's a local woman, Tamara. Tamara Howard.'

'Okay, then.' Robbie regarded Zilla for a second, but couldn't read those shining, shadowed eyes. He flipped a fresh page in his notepad. 'And it appears there are some injuries?'

Zilla nodded, and leaned over to lift one of Ellie's chubby thighs. Her soft skin pulled away from the vinyl, reluctant as a sticker clinging to an overripe plum. The child held her breath, silent hiccups still juddering through her small frame. 'Sh-sh-shh,' Zilla crooned, gently rotating Ellie's leg until Robbie could see the bruises and sticky plasters.

He kept his face blank. 'Is that it?'

Zilla carefully laid Ellie's leg on the seat, placing one firm hand softly on her knee as if sticking it back into place. 'It's all over the back of her legs. Some scratches.' She indicated the First Aid detritus beside them. 'And there's a tear in her dress.'

Robbie stood stock still for a second, then swore quietly. Reaching for his radio, he turned his face towards the wall while he put a request in for support from Child Protection. Yet another strung-out mum had lashed out at her kid, he figured, then done a guilty runner.

He turned back to Zilla. 'We're gonna get a doctor to have a look at her, right? Check she's okay.'

Ellie's face was blotchy from the hiccups. She coughed wetly, snot bubbling from one of her nostrils.

Zilla frowned. 'But she's not okay.'

'Then that's even more reason. There'd have to be a doctor's surgery on site, right?'

'Not anymore. It moved when the Medical Centre opened just across the road, on Bayview Street. We called them half an hour ago. They said they'd send over a doctor as soon as one was free.'

'Nice to know they're giving it priority treatment.' *Bloody amateurs.* 'Call them again, see what's going on. I'm going to have a chat with Ellie here.'

Zilla and Ellie both looked up with close-mouthed shock at the suggestion.

Robbie put out his hand to assist Zilla from the couch. She ignored him, and pushed herself up. Ellie grabbed hold of the front of her dress, bunching it up in both her hands tighter and tighter as Robbie approached.

He paused. 'Zilla, I'm going to need you here. Can you stay in the room while you make the call.'

'Don't worry, I'm not going anywhere.' Zilla drew her phone from her pocket, dialling.

He moved a little closer, squatted down in front of the girl, and spoke very slowly and softly 'Hi there, Ellie. My name's Robbie, and I'm a policeman.'

Nothing.

'Ellie, did you come to the shops with your mother today?'

Still nothing. Behind him, he heard Zilla confirm a Doctor was on the way, and drop her phone on the table. But it rang again straight away, and he shot a glance at the screen. *Zaac.*

Sorry, she mouthed. *My brother.* She cancelled the call and pocketed the phone, looking worried.

He turned back to the girl. 'Ellie, do you know where Mummy is? Did she leave the shops?'

'Muuummmyyyy?' Ellie's answer was more a plea.

'That's right, your Mummy. Did anyone else come with you?'

'Mummy car!' Ellie frowned — with anger or effort, he wasn't sure.

Robbie looked over at Zilla. She was in the middle of the call, but raised one hand helplessly and nodded to him, confirming they had heard that a few times before.

'Okay, okay. So you and Mummy came to the shops in your car?'

Ellie's eyes went wide with terror. 'Mummy car! Mummy car mummy car!'

The kid was screaming. Robbie reared up in surprise, nearly toppling over backwards.

Amid the chaos, the door swung open, Stan moving in as quickly as his short legs could carry him. 'Zilla, answer your bloody radio! I've found something in West Car Park B. There's a huge smear on the gravel, out behind the Video Ezy. It stinks. There's flies swarming all over —' He stopped and swallowed, his ruddy face rapidly losing colour.

Robbie moved his gaze from Stan to Ellie and across to Zilla. She stared at him, her complexion blanched as the cold tile floor.

He reached for his radio again. It looked like he was going to get his first chance to work alongside the Gold Coast CIB.

II.

The evening sands of Kurrigee, drunk on summer sun, rolled warm over low dunes. Spinifex grass sprouted silver rough beneath the girls' wandering bare feet.

'Let's go for a swim.'

'A swim? Now?' Zilla breathed through a pang of worry, blowing out her better judgment through pursed lips. 'Sure.'

They turned down towards the ocean, brimmed with wet sand still mirroring the blood-red glow of a dying sunset. Tammy's tanned skin shone like a church lantern as she stood ankle-deep in the swirling white soup.

'Are you going in?' Zilla asked, sliding her toes into the wet flesh of the shoreline.

Tammy looked up to the first star, pinpointing the darkest blue patch of sky to the east. 'They reckon if it's cloudy, dawn, or dusk, then you're sharkbait.' She took another step into the lacework waves.

Zilla followed. 'Yeah – they say.'

Tammy lifted her wrist and extended her fingers to where Zilla stood. 'Alright, we'll go in together.'

They held hands tight and ran squealing into the water. Cool silk on liquid skin, coiling cold around their feet, crests high enough to smack their half-turned shoulders. A set of six waves moved past the finger-plaited girls as they yelped and yahooed, conquering each in turn.

A lull.

Tammy's hand thrummed with life in Zilla's palm. She heard Tam's lips gently pop, then a musical swish of underwater movement.

'Hey!' Her legs went out from under her, as Tammy's netball-strong thighs wrapped around her own. Zilla's face tilted back as she sank down, submerged to the hairline.

Tammy moved into view above her; eyes soft and clear. 'You look like a water flower. A black poppy, floating in the sea.'

Something moved in Zilla's torso. A painful, thrilling zephyr that was gone before she knew it was there. 'Shut up!' she wriggled her ankles free and swam clear of Tam in two strong sidepaddle strokes.

'Wooooh!' Tam swirled around three times, encircling herself within a curved cage of splash, then dove under, bursting up next to Zilla. 'What do you wanna do tonight? My 'rentals will just be getting blind with yours. Again.'

Zilla couldn't talk about things like Tam could. She could never say that out loud, although it was true: their parents and family friends were drunk nearly all the time on these camping trips. 'Go for a walk?'

Tam smiled as an idea gripped her. 'Let's make it all the way to the Pin tonight.'

They glided into touch, then trod up the beach to the campsite. Low ripstop triangles dotted the ragged outline of their group. The gaslit communal tarp threw shifting shadows, and a flicker of doubt crossed Zilla's heart. Here were family, friends, all the trappings of belonging. Their cheery chatter hadn't deteriorated yet, but she knew it would come. In a couple of hours, rage-fuelled nonsense and bitter silences would fill their corner of the campground.

Was it her fault she hated all of them with every cell in her awkward, morphing body?

At the girls' tent Zilla grabbed a teeshirt, Tam her favourite white sarong. They swooped through the communal area to snitch a lemonade.

'We're going for a walk,' Zilla mumbled, passing behind her Dad's canvas chair.

'You stay near campsite,' Petre slurred carefully. 'You be good girls now.'

She answered with a soft huff, swinging her arms with more force than necessary as she raced to catch up with Tam. Tam didn't ask for permission. For anything.

As they made their way past the last guy-ropes, Zilla heard a movement in the low mulga scrub. She stopped, hissing Tam's name.

They stood still, searching with their eyes. The scrub smelled of dust and disinfectant. After a minute, Tam grabbed her hand and dragged them both into their wandering. 'Hungry goanna, probably.'

'Jumpinpin is an hour away, right?' Zilla knew it from day-long fishing trips in her Dad's runabout, but she'd never been ashore on that northern end of the island, where a narrow break between Kurrigee and Minjerriba allowed wild ocean currents to crash through into the Broadwater.

Tam shrugged. 'An hour or two. Maybe not that far.'

Another rustling bush snagged Zilla's attention. A dirty face peered out at them, dark eyes flinty bright with judgement. Tam groaned. 'Your brother is such a pain.'

'Zaac!' Zilla caught his elbow, holding tight. 'Are you spying on us?'

'Leggo, I'm not!' Zaac squirmed like a skink in her grip. 'But Zilla, you shouldn't go off in the dark.'

'Rack off, kid.' Tam shooed him away like a Queen dismissing a servant.

'It's not safe! You should take me with you.' Zaac puffed out his puny chest. 'For protection!'

Zilla giggled at the sight of him. 'You, protect us?' She used his arm as leverage to pull him close, then push him away, back towards camp. 'Go back to the tent, dickweed!'

Zac backed away, rubbing his elbow. 'Umm-ah, I'm telling!'

'Telling what? We're not doing anything!' Zilla stamping her foot, making as if to chase him.

Zaac turned and picked up his pace.

'Moron!' Tam called after him, then wrapped an arm around Zilla's shoulders. 'Leave him. He'll forget about it in two seconds. And the parents all too far gone to care.'

The girls stood in a silence broken only by the shurush of far-off waves, watching as the scrub and sand around them made the final change into night shadows and shine. As one, they turned their footsteps around and headed north, into the rising moon.

The worn cotton hem of her faded one-piece rubbed Zilla's crotch painfully. Sea-salt sting. She looked around, surreptitiously slipped a finger under the coarse gusset, twitching her bottom on the warm log where she was perched.

Tammy looked completely glamorous across the low, illegal campfire, the soft pyramids of her new, sky-blue lycra bikini shining like pieces of treasure. Her tanned belly rose flat above the white tassels of the sarong draped around her hips. Zilla couldn't tell, looking at her perfect changling silhouette in the flickering light, if Tam was a woman or a girl.

Nor could these guys, she reckoned.

'So, where are you heading on this big adventure, then?'

'Up to the Pin.' Tam lifted her jawline in a proud challenge as the guys guffawed.

'The Pin? That's miles away, you nongs!'

Brad, Zilla thought. The round-faced one with the shoulder-length brown hair and kind eyes; that one's Brad.

'We've already been walking for ages. And Zilla's been there, heaps of times!'

'Who has?'

Tam pointed. 'Zilla.'

Zilla wished she could disappear. Shrink down and crawl into the gaping sandcrab holes, dotted like shot gun damage in the dunes banked around them.

'As in *Godzilla*? What a name!' Sean, the tall one, with narrow muscles and spiky white hair.

'You don't look like a monster,' added Brad quietly, speaking only to her.

But Zilla had always thought maybe she did look like a kind of monster. Daggy old-fashioned clothes, big round bum, and skin that never tanned shiny like a macadamia nut but was either dust white in winter or mud black in summer.

'You reckon you've walked to the Pin, Godzilla?' Sean wouldn't let it go.

Tam jumped to her feet, ready to defend. 'Don't call her that!'

'Hey, settle down.' Sean reached up and stroked Tam's elbow, placating, guiding her back to the spot on his log. 'I was only joking.'

'I've been up to the Pin heaps of times.' Zilla's cheeks tingled with a shy blush. 'Only by boat, but.'

'You've got a boat? What sort?' Brad looked impressed.

'My Dad's got a —'

'It's a red runabout, and it's a beauty.' Tam smiled, her white teeth shining like a sliver moon. 'Zilla can drive it.'

'Aye, aye, Cap'n!' Brad saluted her, and Sean broke out in rough-throated laughter. He passed a dirty orange juice bottle over to Brad. It stank like the cow dung Zilla's cousins burned on Uncle Szynka's farm; foul and sweet and forbidden. She knew what it was; drawn and repelled, fascinated, she watched intently as Brad inverted a lighter into its stem, pulled bubbles for a full minute, then held his breath until his eyes popped.

'Want a cone?' Sean asked Tam.

'Sure.' Tam made it sound like she'd had a million of them, and didn't really care one way or the other. Like it was no biggie.

But Zilla knew it was a biggie.

There was a line in the sand, literally, and they had come up at it so suddenly, so unexpectedly. Completely unprepared; no time to put their heads together and make a plan. Both she and Tam were now taut arrows, bow-stretched towards what was on the other side of that line, but Zilla alone was held paralysed at what it would make of them.

Sean packed a tiny pinch of hazel leaf into the stem, and passed it to Tam. Holding out a flame with chivalrous care, his eyes caught the light like a wild dog's. Tam's collarbones floated high, her bare ribs expanding under the tiny shiny triangles of her bikini top. Zilla's core cramped with jealousy. Sean was so good-looking; broad cheekbones and an even smile and narrow hips, flecks of white gold here and there where boyish body hair hugged his lean curves.

A couple of seconds at the juice bottle, then a loud click as the charred lump pulled through the stem. Tam jerked away, her lungs exploding with smoke and voiceless shock.

'You want one, Captain?' Brad's soft voice tugged her attention gently away. Zilla froze. She had nothing, not one moment from her whole life, to offer her a way to respond. So she reverted to her baseline: *I am not worth it*. She pulled her dry lips apart to answer, when Sean interrupted.

'Her?' He measured her with his gaze, from frizz to flat chest to feet and up again. 'She's not old enough.'

Zilla took a breath. This is where Tam jumped in, every time.

Silence.

Tam sat slumped, her eyes open but unseeing, focus turned completely within. The corner of her lips tweaked; a smile or a grimace.

Zilla realized she was completely alone, predators' teeth thrilling at her neck. Her bones hollowed. She ached for experience, acceptance, even admiration.

But experience alone would do.

'I — I — I'm a year younger than Tam. That's all.'

'And how old is the lovely Tam?' Sean leant his palm softly on Tam's thigh, right in the middle where muscles turned soft and sensitive. Her eyes brightened a shade in response, and a full smile formed.

Zilla watched, something warming between her own thighs; a crazy buzzing that seemed to flow from her very centre, out along energy lines she never knew she had, and into every cell. A light breeze lifted the tail of her hair; a flapping sound caught her attention. She glanced towards the guys' tent, a pale green dome with a black mesh mouth filled with the promise of dirt and danger.

'I'm sixteen,' said Tam, her voice a bent husk. Sexy laryngitis.

'Sixteen, hey? Only a few years younger than us.' Sean wagged his finger to and fro a few times, then paused as he, too, glanced at the tent.

Sixteen? A fist squeezed Zilla's heart.

Brad was looking at her, curious and distant. 'Sean.' One word, a warning.

The tent mouth loomed, beckoning. Zilla's mind wandered, into the tent and far beyond the scope of her imagination.

Sean leaned in further towards Tam. Her eyelids dropped, slow as a roller door, head tipping back a fraction under its own weight.

Zilla's heart kicked into action, a painful spasm pummelling her chest. There was a place deep inside the far reaches of her mind, a safe room; a place she had built over the years as her parents drank and drank, and Ma picked fights with Dad until tears darkened his eyelashes and made him look weirdly pretty. She found that place now. Ran in, slammed the door shut, pulled the curtains, flicked off the lights.

Hidden, she peeked out.

Sean's face was right next to Tam's; her lips slipped apart just enough to see her front teeth glisten. Sean bent forward to close the gap; Zilla saw his elbow bend as his hand shaped into an empty cup. Explorative fingertips moved in slowly, unnoticed, as if under a radar. The exact moment his lips made soft contact with Tam's, his gentle tentacles brushed one of those bright blue triangles, back and forth, so softly that Zilla wondered if Tam even noticed.

A delicate bump rose under the thin blue lycra. Zilla slicked her tongue across her teeth, tasting sweet hard musk. Moisture formed in the corners of her mouth as she watched Sean's palm close around Tam's bikini, his thumb moving in slow circles. He gave a soft, deep, uncontrolled grunt, right into Tam's open mouth.

Zilla twitched on the log as she had before, longing to slip a finger under her worn cotton gusset again — to rearrange, and press, and explore. Her breath came fast and light, barely there at all.

Not worth it.

Lightheaded, heavy limbed, Zilla was hauled from her darkened room. Her toes scrunched painfully into the cold sand beneath the surface. She checked around, disoriented, suddenly terrified.

'You'd better go.' Brad was looking at her, right at her face, his kind eyes fierce with judgment; a teacher giving a final warning before handing out detentions.

A dart of guilt stung her into action. 'Tam, Tam. We've gotta go.' Zilla backed away from the logs, from the faded tent. 'Tammy!'

Brad stumbled around the campfire mound. 'Sean, the girls have to go.'

Sean and Tam slowly moved apart, as if bound by invisible cobweb. Zilla sought out her friend's eyes, pleading.

Tam's face snapped shut. 'Fuck's sake, Zilla.'

'Do you really have to go?' Sean reached again for Tam's thigh.

But this time, Tam looked over at Brad and twitched her leg away, masking the movement as she stood to go. 'Yeah, thanks for the ...' she trailed off, her fine fingers waving slowly to take in the fire, the log, everything. 'Seeya another time, maybe.'

She floated towards the narrow pathway leading into the scraggly mulga scrub.

'See you later then, the lovely Tam.' Sean ran his broad hands through his hair then linked them behind his neck, watching her drift away. His lips pursed into a private smile. 'It was very, very nice to meet you.'

Zilla moved quickly, grabbing Tam's hand and pulling her away. She couldn't stand the thought of the guys' eyes on her for one more second, and she didn't want to leave any chance for Tam to change her mind, turn back.

Tam leaned her weight against Zilla's forward momentum, and tipped her face up into the moonlight. 'I feel funny.'

Zilla glanced over her shoulder. In a silvery puzzle piece between twisted branches, she could see the guys laughing and shaking their heads as Sean adjusted the centre seam of his boardshorts. Her thoughts flew off into the unknown again, a thick flock of bats, turbulent and ravenous.

She stayed quiet until they were out of earshot.

'That was fun, hey.' Tam's hand relaxed into Zilla's, palms merging into a familiar clasp as they strolled along the moonlit path.

'Yeah, it was okay.'

Tam's free hand played with the knot in her sarong, resting it perfectly snug in the curve below her hipbone. She looked at Zilla for the first time since she'd put her lips to the dirty orange juice bottle; raised her eyebrows, and smiled.

Tam moved so slowly it was a miracle they made it to their campsite, and she kept up a low, hazy chatter the whole time. Zilla couldn't understand most of it: sometimes so outrageous she'd laugh along, but mostly boring, in a scary kind of way.

'I'm hungry,' Tam said for the hundredth time.

Nightmarish silhouettes flickered in the communal area — some of the grownups were still in action. Zilla spied her mother's form, leering threateningly over a seated stranger. She spun around, grabbed Tam's hand again, and pulled her towards their tent.

'I'm really, really hungry. Let's get something to eat.' Tam picked up a handful of her sungold hair, chomping and giggling into it. 'Something to eeeeeeeat.'

Zilla stopped, keeping a firm hold on Tam's hand. 'You can't go in there like this. They'll know.'

'As if.' Tam pulled free of Zilla's grip and marched straight towards the kitchen tarp, all business. But once she reached the boxes of food, she fell into reverie, swaying gently over multi-coloured plastic choices.

Zilla rushed in, grabbed a big packet of chips and a Coke, nudging Tam with her hip. 'Okay, let's go.'

Her mother glanced their way, narrowing her eyes. She wore heavy make-up and shapeless crocheted bikinis. Zilla could see Ma's lips move, but she ducked her head and waved. 'G'night, everyone.'

'Night, girls,' drawled a few of the people nearest. Tam's Mum and Zilla's Dad were sitting side-by-side on the big esky, deep in conversation. Zilla froze for a second, caught in a snapshot glance at Dad's hairy thigh pressed alongside Tam's Mum's.

A tug on her hand broke her train of thought.

They ran to their tent. Zilla expertly arced the zipper door open in one motion, and let Tam through before stepping in and zipping it shut. Zilla flopped on her sleeping bag, tingling with liberation at having reached their own private hideaway, and let herself laugh. Tam fell beside her, rolling in to giggle softly in her ear, her curved body twitching with glee. Zilla pulled open the chips and held it out to her, setting off a feeding frenzy that lasted until the packet was empty. She cracked the Coke and took a sip, passing it to Tam who finished it in six gulps.

Burrrp. 'God, that feels better.' Tam's voice was clear. She flipped onto her back, lifting her legs to tickle the tent ceiling with her toes. *Fzzzt, fzzzt.*

'What was it like?'

Tam's eyes sparkled in the darkness. 'It was amazing.' Her hand stroked her forearm, then lazily unknotted her sarong. 'He was a really good kisser. But I though I was going to throw up from the smoke, and I was just petrified, trying to hold it in!' She laughed again; a normal, Tam-sounding laugh.

'You didn't look petrified.' Zilla heard the resentment in her own voice. 'You looked really beautiful. No wonder he wanted to kiss you.'

'Really? Did I?'

'But you said you were sixteen!'

'Of course. Or else he wouldn't have kissed me.'

They lay side by side, a wave building up inside Zilla. The pressure trapped air in her lungs, forcing a whisper. 'When he kissed you, he touched your boob.'

'What?' Tam leant up on one elbow. 'He did not!'

'He did, I saw it.'

'Where? Show me.'

Zilla reached out her hand, fingers mimicking the explorative tentacles still dazzling her memory. 'Really?'

Tam's breath puffed out in soft spurts. She closed her eyes. 'Show me where he touched me.'

Zilla's calf muscles locked up, toes flexed hard to control the pace of her hand curling slowly towards Tam's bikini. When the sensitive tips of her fingers made contact, a loud pop sounded, deep in her brain. Her thoughts scattered with the rush of blood compressing her throat.

Tam wedged her thumb between her own legs, twisting her wrist slowly. 'You be Sean.' She rolled onto her back, her voice a hiss filling the small, musty tent. 'You be him, and I'll be me.'

Zilla swallowed, unsure of her voice. 'I want you to be me.'

'What?'

'I'll be Sean, if you be me.'

Tam sighed, knuckles pulsing on her crotch. 'Alright, I'm you.'

Zilla could tell she was lying, but her body was gripped in a tidal pull and she wouldn't argue in case she scared the moment away. Her closed lips were cool and awkward against Tam's, but her hips moved with strength and grace. Finding Tam's. Finding rhythm. Bumping and rubbing; bone against flesh against bone.

'Sean, Sean,' mumbled Tam, playing her part. She clenched her bum cheeks, then released; clenched, and released, angling and opening her thighs.

Images flickered through Zilla's mind like passing headlights: Sean's fingers on Tam's nipple, tears staining Dad's eyelashes, the thick pull of surf currents in her hair, Brad's soft jawline set firm with judgment, the lace fringe of Tam's sarong. She pushed forward to lay her entire body on top of Tammy, resting her chin in the cup of her collarbone, the whole world pivoting around the warmest point of contact between them. Everything zoomed away, leaving a cleanswept landscape filled only with the desire to reach the dark, pure line where the sea met the sky. Infinitely far, impossibly close, the talons of shame at her heels.

· · ·

Fine white sand grated in every crevice, alien skin against nylon tent floor. Zilla rotated a fingertip in the pink of her eyes.

Thirsty.

Tam slept on top of her sleeping bag, sarong pulled up over one leg, fists and chin up and away, shadow-boxing. Zilla glanced away, stepped outside. Zipped the door closed on the night.

The latent heat of the day stalked ankle-high dewy succulents, tiny yellow faces blinking from the cold snap dawn. Zilla stumbled, clumsy and half-wake, over tent ropes strung with wet towels. Things were disordered under the communal tarp — upended camp chairs and empty stubbies strewn around — but the food was neatly packed away. Zilla hefted a water bag onto the esky and found a cup.

She needed to go.

The bushes flashed silver below, green above, and red-brown spikes all over. She followed the narrow path, cool sand massaging her bare feet. Her favourite spot was deep in the scrub; a little hollow surrounded by golden banksia. She peed straight into an ant hole, enjoying her aim. A flutter above her head, an olive bird honking quiet laughter. *Takadok, takadok.*

She smiled. Early, early morning, before anyone else was up to mess with her day.

No need to rush back; it was Zilla's time to wander. Alone with the sky. Free. She turned her steps away from the Broadwater into the thickest part of the island, exploring a new way across to the surf side. A flat, brown teatree pond glinted between the scrub. She found a way through and carefully smoothed a place to kneel on the muddy bank. Scrunched up her nose, and dipped her head all the way over so that her hair cascaded in. Splashed her face. She straightened, and twisted the strands into a plait held in place by its own wet weight. The stink of teatree water was bad, but it left you feather soft.

Awake, senses open, she pressed on. She hungered for the deepest blue, drawn to the caress of wave breaks. Not far now.

A rusted shed threw a soft grey ghost over her path, a relic from a fisherman's lease before this place became a national park. It was tall and wide as a big, big man. She slowed, a chill running over her. The corrugated flap doorway lay open a crack into a world of cobwebby gloom that didn't belong here, in her dawn paradise.

Did something move in there?

She found a toehold along the crumbling edge of the iron door, and opened it a touch wider. Her eyes began to adjust to the dark within. Something was definitely inside, wedged against a thick block of wood on the cracked concrete floor. In fact, the floor was covered with strange shapes back there, wall to wall.

Zilla curved her spine, pressed the door open a little further, thighs beginning to quiver from brolga balancing.

A shard of bone-white, here and there, amidst some oil-smeared, umm, fur was it? Was that grey fur and mulberries, maybe? A drunken, feasting possum?

She leaned a fraction closer. Her foot slipped in its grip against the serrated edge of the door. A cap of pink skin tore loose from her big toe. The pain sliced through her. But the gasp of shock locked in her windpipe as her eyes resolved the shadows into shapes.

The flattened corpse of a mother cat. Arced, still protective, around a pool of destroyed kittens. Blood and guts and brain, clumped and wet on shredded fur. A fungal, mean stink curled around them.

The big chunk of wood lay across the mother's skull: murder weapon, coffin.

And amidst it all a tiny paw, still twitching. The fine pierce of claws extending, retracting, extending.

The scream built in Zilla for a long minute before it blew the dam wall at her throat, sending birds up from the scrub in a shock wave of sound to the high blue sky.

Everything was moving; too fast to see, too fast to feel. Leaf spikes scraping her cheeks, sand in her blooded toe. Nothing, nothing. Pure, formless motion. Tripwire ropes clutching her foot, throwing her on the ground. Up. Movement. Nothing.

Her Mother.

'Druzcilla, slow down. What is – ack, your foot. Stop!'

Ma's cold fingernails in her shoulder flesh, Ma's smeared lipstick making familiar, meaningless sounds.

Zilla shuddered out a word, two. Pointed into the shadows of the scrub. 'Dead. All dead.' Not safe yet, but far enough from danger for the first tears to form.

Her mother's skinny behind, marching off along the narrow path. Zilla stood stock still, anchored with terror. Her mind began to pose questions, between the nightmare flashes of broken pingpong skulls; questions she couldn't fathom, answers she couldn't consider.

'Zilla, come with!'

Jerked into action, following Ma, eyes on the leaf litter barbed like Ninja stars. 'My toe,' she mumbled, the dull ache seeping in.

'First we see.'

'I can't.' She stopped, pointed past the pond to the shed, camouflaged in rust brown bush. 'I can't look.'

'Tsch.' Her mother's jutted her elbows and stalked off.

And for a minute, nothing. Bleeding pain. Questions without answers.

Ma burst from the bushes, fingers reaching for Zilla's hair, eyes blank with mindless rage. 'What have you done?'

She tangled and pulled, dragging Zilla back to camp. 'You do this, and you show it to me? *U bent in de problemen nu, meisje.* Big trouble.'

Zilla bunkered down, deep in her basement room, as a maelstrom of mangled language tore at her nerves. Ma marched her to their tent, unzipping it hard and fast. Dad emerged, bleary eyes confused, trying to understand, to reason.

Wilde!

Dziki?

Feral.

'I saw that woman last night. I saw you. And now you are here with no sleep and this daughter, who is just like you.' Ma was all starburst accusations, pinching out punishments. 'No more, Petre. We go home now. Never again.'

Adults arguing. A couple of men of men heading off with a sack and a shovel, muttering about a decent burial. Someone sitting Zilla on a stump, pouring water over her toe, pressing too hard on a Band-Aid that refused to stick. Eventually, the fuss died down a little, and Zilla was left alone to sip a warm can of lemonade.

Behind the communal tarp, she spied a six-year old spectre. Watching, mouth small and shut below sparking eyes. Zilla saw him, and in that moment, her little brother became the focal point for all the hatred she could never show Ma and Dad. 'Zaac, did you do that to the cats, you little shit?'

'No, I never!' He shook his head so hard, his hands jangled.

'Sure you didn't. Piss off, weirdo. Stop spying on me.'

For a second, his young face faltered under the weight of her gaze. But then he puffed out his chest like he'd done the night before. 'I told you it wasn't safe.'

'Like you could have done anything to help. You're not

Superman, you know.' She punctuated the words with vicious stabs of her finger in the air. 'You're a useless little kid.'

He shook his head at her, *no*, and disappeared.

Her toe throbbed, echoing the throb between her legs last night, and she nearly moaned with shame. She took another sip of lemonade, and closed her eyes.

III.

Zilla's skin was hardening to linoleum in the stale air con. If she didn't get a break from the First Aid room soon, she'd disappear, camouflaged perfectly into the beige vinyl couch and salmon-pink walls. But she couldn't and wouldn't leave Ellie's side.

She watched as Doctor Gow's thin latex gloves wielded a cotton bud delicately as a calligraphy pen, swabbing with excruciating care across the tiny torn fingertips. 'You bite your nails, hey?' The doctor addressed Ellie gently, breaking his steadfast professional mask for the first time. 'My daughter did too, all the way 'til she was a big girl of twelve.' He bagged and tagged the bud then spoke quietly to Zilla, on duty as supervisor until they could rustle up a female cop in the District.

'That's all for now. She's fine to travel. I want her taken straight to Southport Hospital. They'll finish the exam and provide care until we find a family member.'

'The police are in touch with the grandmother. She's on her way here.'

'The child's dress shows signs of rough handling, but I'll leave it for the Response Unit to process.'

Ellie, stone still since the Doctor arrived, lifted one plump little hand to the shoulder strap of her dress, grasping the bow in a tired pincer grip and moving it closer to her neck. A small, futile gesture of self-protection.

Rough handling. Empathy spilled through Zilla's chest, but she held her face carefully blank.

'I assume the grandmother has been instructed to supply a change of clothes?' Doctor Gow twisted his lips in distrust of all intellect but his own.

'I don't know. You'll need to talk to Constable Farquhari.'

She willed him to leave, aching to move over and comfort the silent, slumped girl.

There was a single rap at the door. A grey-haired lady with a broom-handle spine stepped into the room.

'Gamma?' Ellie spoke for the first time in more than an hour.

'Come here, Elle.' Her manner was oddly formal, showing no evidence of concern or sympathy. When Zilla looked into those ice blue eyes, she saw a woman from a generation that equated feelings with weakness.

'Beverly Howard.' She turned her cold gaze to Doctor Gow. 'I have spoken with Detective Sergeant Hutchens, and he agrees — it would be best if I take Elle to the hospital. The Constable can follow in his car.'

Doctor Gow blinked as though someone had flicked water in his face. 'Are you the missing woman's mother?'

'No. The child's father is my son.' A frown flickered across her gaze. She shook it off, lifting her eyebrows and looking at the Doctor through half-lowered lids. 'And Tamara isn't missing. There's obviously just been a terrible mix-up. She's a — she has had problems in the past, you know.'

Through the open door, Zilla could see Farquhari watching the scene through squinted eyes, pocketing his mobile phone.

'I'm afraid you'll need to wait for Child Protection.'

Doctor Gow was kind, but firm. 'They'll require an Officer —'

Farquhari stepped into the doorway, his tone flat with suppressed frustration. 'No, she's cleared to escort the child. I've just confirmed it with my OIC.'

Doctor Gow nodded his head, processing this new arrangement. 'Well, I'll see you at Southport Hospital, then.'

'Actually, we are going to Jacaranda Private.' Beverly held up one hand, as the other reached to grasp Ellie's outstretched fingers. 'I have contacted the family physician, and he is on his way there to meet the paediatrician from Child Protection.'

Farquhari frowned. He glanced over at Zilla as if for backup, but what could either of them do? His boss had spoken. 'Thanks for your assistance, Doc. We'll be in touch. The family will take care of the girl from here.'

'Right.' Doctor Gow looked uncertain for a second, eyes tracing the shapes around the small room as if he had misplaced his keys. Then he picked up his bag, frowning at Beverly Howard as if he suspected the family might be the whole problem, and left.

Beverly and Ellie followed next, making their way down the corridor; a mismatched pairing of determination and trepidation, order and chaos. Zilla followed slowly, a thick rubber band binding her to the girl, stretching painfully as they walked further away. She wanted to say goodbye; to reassure Ellie everything would be okay, even though she was numb with fear that everything had gone terribly, terribly wrong.

'Ms. Bannich?' Farquhari caught up to her next to the empty Security Control Office, gesturing inside. 'Zilla?'

Zilla slowed her steps, reluctant to let Ellie out of her sight. But Robbie loomed in her peripheral vision; the breadth of his shoulders, the lift of his cheekbone. He seemed agitated, off his stride, not the confident cop who'd first entered the First Aid room. He bent his body slightly towards her, conspiratorial, as he gave her his card.

'I'll need to speak to you. At the station.'

She took it with clumsy fingers. 'You need to interview me?'

'Well, I'll need a statement.' He bent closer, trying to catch her gaze. 'At least.'

Zilla sighed, and shrugged her shoulders in agreement. 'Alright. But I'm exhausted, and I've got to get home to — there's something I've got to do. I can be at the station by six, okay?'

Ahead, a hydraulic hiss. Zilla stepped into the corridor just in time to see Ellie's face scrunch up as she stepped into the brightly lit mall, her grandmother's hand pulling her forward briskly now, so that she nearly tripped. The heavy door thudded shut.

Zilla's blood pressure fell away, and cold sweat prickled her brow. She fought a swoon. Robbie was saying something to her.

'What?'

'Nothing. Just, how did you know the mother's name? Did one of the Samaritans know the girl or something?'

Zilla put one hand on the wall for support, forcing her mind clear of the storm clouds forming. 'Ellie's name was written on the inside of her shoe. I worked it out from there. Tamara Howard was a friend of the family, years ago.' Her voice lowered, broken with memories of the splintering rift, the long ache of absence. And then, that one phone call. 'But I haven't seen Tammy Parry in years.'

'Hey, you don't look well. Are you going to be okay?' He touched her elbow, solicitous. 'I know this is — well, a lost child is always stressful, but if you knew the mother ...'

'I'm alright. Like I said, it was years ago.'

'I'll see you at the station later, then.' He moved his head until he could see her eyes. 'Good job today, Zilla.'

No, not really. Not at all. 'Thanks, Robbie.'

'Druzcilla, what time is it?' The quiver in her mother's tone might have been from age, rage, or sunset effect. It didn't matter. Zilla's answer was always the same.

'I'm just home from work, Ma. Let me wash up, and I'll make a quick supper.' She pushed the front door closed against the resistance of once plush carpet, now wrinkled and frayed, and stuck her head around the corner into the lounge room. It was as dim as a crypt, stinking of wet dog and vinegar. 'Any visitors today?'

'Who'd come?' Marja lifted the remote, her wrist writhing gracefully as an eel, and clicked the wrong button once, twice. The volume climbed until they both winced. 'Mute, mute! Rotten bugger.'

'What's that fucking *noise*?' A sliding door scraped along dust-worn tracks, and Zilla's brother Izaac came in from the canal front. A red cattle dog followed him and dashed for the couch, jumping up and curling in before anyone could call him off.

'Language, please, Zaaci.'

Zaac slouched over to his mother's recliner. Grabbed the remote, hit mute, and caught Zilla's reflection in the television screen. He turned, and froze.

They stared each other down over Marja's head. Zaac wore faded boardies that barely clung to his skinny hips, and an unbuttoned flannel shirt, sleeves rolled to half-mast. His bare feet, black with mangrove mud, had tracked marks across the room.

'What are *you* doing here?' Zilla's rage at her brother was old and so familiar, pumping through her like venal blood, worthless and vital. It defined her. Resenting her brother, mourning her Dad, and taking care of her Ma — they had become the trinity of touchstones for her own identity. This, the only place she belonged, was the last place she wanted to be.

Especially today.

Zaac broke eye contact, shrugged. 'I'm starving. What's for dinner?'

She glared at his half-turned cheek. 'Come give me a hand, and you'll find out.'

Zaac unmuted the tele and reset the volume. Zilla moved into the narrow kitchen, and he joined her reluctantly. She moved with swift automatic efficiency: homebrand wholemeal bread, margarine, ham, cheese, a smear of pale yellow mustard — sliced and stacked in the time it took Zaac to root around in the overhead cupboards that screened them from Marja.

He put his favourite glass down on the bench, and crossed behind Zilla to pull a beer from the fridge. 'Want one?'

Her whole body jerked in fury, the butter knife spinning out of her fingers and skittering along the bench. She slammed her palm on it before it hit the floor. 'I have to go down to the station.'

'Police?' Zaac blinked his sandy lashes rapidly, as if trying to clear his vision. 'When? What happened?'

Zilla channelled all her resentment into a glowering stare, deploying her heavy brow to full effect.

'Fuck off, I been driving all day. I had to get —'.

'I know, Zaac. But why did you come back here?'

'Who's in trouble with the Police?' Marja surprised them both, appearing in the doorway. She rested one hand high on the doorframe to support herself, loose folds of skin at her wrist twisting with the effort. 'Zaaci?'

'It's not me, Ma! Zill has to go talk to them.'

'Druzcilla.' Ma's tone was layered with years of suspicion, and weighted with satisfaction. Finally, her willful girl was bearing the blame her golden haired boy had always unfairly attracted.

'There was an incident at work today, that's all. I have to go and give a statement.'

Zaac rubbed an ochre-stained fingertip over his chapped lips, watching his sister's face.

'What happened?' Marja's voice, thin and broken as it was, could still cut leather.

'A toddler was found. A little girl.' Zilla swallowed painfully, the memory of Ellie's thighs making her gut clench. 'She has some injuries. No sign of the mother.'

Silence coiled against the kitchen tiles like a snake.

'Shit.' Zaac finally commented, avoiding Zilla's eyeline. 'Bad scene.'

'Ack.' Marja turned away. 'Parents today, they have no idea. Terrible, terrible.'

Zilla clamped her gorge against the retorts that rose like bile. Marja moved back to the lounge, muttering a string of invectives against *parents today* that Zilla knew would spiral into generalised paranoia and, later that night, the compulsive hoarding of imagined treasures. She reached for the medicine shelf above the fridge.

'Here, make sure she takes these after her sandwich.' She grabbed a bubble-pack strip from a box and popped out two orange capsules. 'And give her a cup of tea.'

'Zill?' He looked at her blankly, sounding six years old. That little boy who always spied on her, followed her, dobbed her in. 'I'm sorry. When she — I couldn't — I didn't know what else to do. I just did what you said.'

'You fucked up, Zaac. Everything's fucked up.' She drew his hand to hers and dropped the capsules into his palm, then held it for a moment, squeezing his knuckles hard. Intending to hurt. 'Just stay here for now, stay with Ma. Watch tele. I've gotta go change.' She dropped his hand, heading for the unlit hallway to her room.

'Zill, the copper.' Zaac turned his back to her as he looked out over the turgid canal. His bony shoulders were scrunched halfway up his neck like a sand anchor under the thin flannel shirt. 'Is it ... anyone we know?'

'Nah.' She waited for him to look at her, then held up one thumb in a small shared gesture of hope. 'It's a new guy.'

Runaway Bay Police Station had only been built recently, its smooth plaster façade in marked contrast to the rough orange brick of buildings either side. Two Bangalow palms, sturdy and clean, stood sentinel by the entrance. Technically evening, the sun still shone hot and high. Zilla's bare arms were sticky with sweat, chafing where her tank top gaped a little at the sides.

She'd walked the five blocks over. Hungry, exhausted, uncomfortable, she wanted to get the interview over and done with. At home, hidden behind the frozen dinners, was a bag of rock hard Cherry Ripes with her name on it; her reward for making it through this day.

Robbie Farquhari was one of only two cops on duty. He escorted her into the station breakroom, made her a cup of sweet tea, and showed her a seat at one end of the big blondewood table. He pulled his chair up to the corner next to her so they sat side by side, still able to see each other's faces.

'Have you ever dealt with anything like this before?'

She shook her head. 'No way, never.'

'How long have you been at the centre?'

'A couple of years.'

'You seem kind of young.' He cleared his throat, and she

suddenly wondered if he was shy, underneath. 'Ah, for that job, I mean.'

'Working in Security is a steady income. The hours are good. I have stuff I need to take care of, outside work.' She lifted her eyes to the ceiling; a downlight instantly burnt a cigarette hole in her retina. 'My Mother has Parkinson's.'

Robbie nodded and made a soft, sympathetic sound. He seemed exhausted, too. His light brown, curly hair had finally surrendered to the heat of the day, lying flat across his skull.

Zilla took a sip of her drink, waiting for her vision to clear. 'How's Ellie?'

'Haven't heard since she got to hospital. The family doctor is refusing to deal with anyone but the boss.'

She thought about it for a second. 'Hutchens?'

Robbie finally raised his eyes and looked at her, surprised. 'Yeah, Detective Sergeant Hutchens. How do you — do you know him?'

'You mentioned him today — the grandmother, remember? Anyway, at this end of the Coast —' Zilla shrugged '— it's a little village. Everyone knows everyone. Except now there's a whole bunch of new people, too, of course. Moving in.'

'How long have you lived here?'

'Me? Always. I've always lived here.'

'Oh, right. Sorry, I just assumed. With your accent.'

'I grew up speaking mostly Dutch at home, and some Polish, but I've been speaking English since before kindergarten.' Zilla bit her words, offended.

'Sorry.' Robbie extended a hand, almost like he wanted to shake on it. 'I'm not usually — I know what it's like. Family.'

'Yes. Family.'

They observed each other over their mugs of tea for a moment.

'Speaking of family, any news about Ellie's? Have you — have you found her Mum?'

Robbie's brows contracted, sketching lines of concern across his face. 'We're hopeful of a sighting. Once we get the word out.'

'When will that be? Wouldn't it have to be soon, so that it's still fresh in people's minds?'

'Sure. But the Howards are not keen to release any information at this stage. They are understandably distressed over what happened to Ellie, and they all seem convinced that the Mother is off somewhere, recovering from a bender. So my boss needs to go through the correct process with them. It takes time.'

'You've in touch with the rest of the family now?'

'Yeah. The grandmother you met, plus the missing woman's parents. And the husband, Tony Howard. He's up at the hospital, I think.'

'So that prick is still around.'

'You know him, too?'

'Nope, but like I said, it's a small town. I've heard of him.' The skin on Zilla's face tightened. 'And I know he's good mates with Billy Hutchens.'

Robbie blinked in surprise. 'Really?'

'Yep.'

His frown deepened. Zilla's right hand twitched with an impulse to reach over and run her fingertips along the horizontal creases in his forehead. She breathed through the moment, sitting still so as not to disturb the downhill flow of his thoughts.

'Why did you call Howard a prick?'

She laid her forearms on the table, blue vein deltas at her wrists pulsing with the vulnerability of truth. 'Because he is, and everyone around here knows it. Pull his records and see for yourself. Been charged a few times with bashing his wife, but he's never once been convicted.' She glanced up under her eyelids and watched Robbie's face as he processed that one.

It took a long moment. But then his mouth hardened, his eyes deepened. 'Really.' This time, it wasn't a question.

'Yeah.' She flipped her left wrist so her watch faced up. 'Look, thanks for the tea. But it's been a really long, crappy day. What do you need from me?'

'Right.' Robbie skulled the last of his drink and pushed the mug away. 'I've spoken to the Jennings family from the Food Court, who found the girl. And your colleague, Stan, and Doctor Gow. You're the last name on my list today — Hutchens is determined to get contemporaneous notes on this one, because the media will be all over it.'

'Huh?'

The hint of a smile lifted his moustache as he tilted to one side, pulled the small, spiral bound notebook from his pocket, and flapped it like a wad of dollars. 'It's all time-stamped. What you say to me now is worth twice as much as what you might say tomorrow, and it drops away exponentially each day after that.'

'Worth what? Who to?'

His smile faded. 'As evidence, Zilla. In court.'

Zilla leaned on the curved edge of the table, and dropped her face into her hands. Her elbows slipped, forcing her to snap her neck taut.

Robbie's voice was kind and cautious. 'Most of what happened today — from your perspective — we've been through it. I've got nearly everything I need.'

'Okay,' Zilla mumbled, face still smothered in her palms.

'But I have to check something — something that Debbie Jennings said. When you first found Ellie, did you — did Ellie hug you?'

'What do you mean?' Zilla's shoulders sank, heavy and unmoving.

'Did you invite the child to have close personal contact?'

'I — I — don't now how to answer that.' She tried to hold her voice steady, but it climbed to the harsh singsong she recognised from her mother. 'Ellie was so upset, she was frozen like a little — like a tiny solid scream. You make it sound — what do you mean *invite*?'

'Look, it's nothing, don't worry.' He slid one hand across the table towards her. 'Don't stress. You were great today — what a nightmare, but overall, you handled it great.'

Zilla sat still, waiting for the blow to fall.

'But, there's just this one thing I need from you. Debbie reported that the child fought against you a little, when you comforted her — maybe even scratched you? And you administered the First Aid, too. I'm going to need a DNA sample.'

She flexed her ankles in an unconscious move for escape. Her chair screeched across the floor. 'What?'

'It's standard procedure. To eliminate you from any evidence found on the child — under her nails, wherever. We can do it here, or you can go to your local doctor tomorrow and have them arrange it. It's only, you know —', he pointed to his own gumline, healthy and pink under stubble-dark cheeks, '— from your mouth. And your hair.'

A cyclone blew through her mind, sucking gravity and scattering her thoughts, but she managed to pull together a response. 'No problem. I'll go see my GP tomorrow. Will you guys pay?'

'Of course. Bring us the receipt, I'll take care of it.'

'Good.' She pushed her chair all the way out and grabbed her bag from the floor. Stretched her lips into a light smile. 'I'll bring you the bill for my haircut, too.'

'Well, alright then.' He grinned. 'I'll walk you out.'

The evening had grown mango soft. Under the palms, Robbie stopped, something about his body language inviting Zilla to pause as well.

She didn't want to go home.

'You hungry?' Robbie didn't look at her when he asked.

'Starving.'

'Great.' He grinned, pointed at driveway running along the side of the Station. 'I'm parked out the back.'

A thrill licked up her spine. She followed him along the clean concrete line, into the darkness. Their movement triggered a floodlight sensor: Robbie's long, lean shadow lay at her feet. She stepped forward into it, her blood thick with the magnetic pull of one more in a long, long line of risks.

'Stop!' Tam woke in a carpeted coffin, yelling at Ellie to get off the road. Jerked her torso upright, knocking her skull against a low metal bar.

Ellie wasn't there.

'You're awake.' A voice floated towards her, muffled but clear.

Pain spiked her hip and shoulder, crushed under her own weight. She straightened her legs an inch, rage flooding her arteries. 'Let me out!'

'We're nearly there.'

The suspension creaked and rocked under her, cracking the fine bones in her neck. Blistering with frustration, she braced her palms against the waffled metal hood, pocked with rubber stoppers and wire brackets. Her eyes found a plastic clamp attached to a long, thin lever. Followed it all the way along to locking mechanism. Her fingers reached for the stiff lever, pulling desperately. 'I have to get out!'

The car swerved, a sudden shift in momentum jamming her head against the wheel hub. 'Stay where you are.'

That high monotone paralysed her.

Tapping sounds; tyres throwing grit against her eardrums. Time clamped and rolled and pulled at her sanity, like every time her husband had her trapped, beaten down and bruised. She screamed in terror.

'Settle down! I think I can see the turnoff — it's just up ahead.'

Her fingers scrabbled around for purchase. Landed on a tight, hard tube, like a bankroll of coins. Dry tears pricked her sinus. Lollies. She sliced one free with her thumbnail, slotted it between her hot, dry lips. Her tonsils ached as glucose crept down her throat.

The car pitched and yawed over rough terrain. A few final heaves then it stopped dead, throwing her against the rear of the back seats. The driver killed the engine, the silence speaking volumes.

'This is it.'

As the boot opened, so did her heart. She sat up, climbed out slowly, sore in every muscle and joint. But hope took hold. Even though everything was wrong: there was no small hand in her hand, the light hurt like needles, the bushland's caustic breath flamed her cheeks. No one knew where she was.

No one knew where she was.

Freedom tore around inside her like freshly washed dogs.

She stumbled as she reached back for her tote. A bony hand steadied her, then grabbed the bag and passed it over. 'I'm sorry. I tried to catch her.'

'You had to let her go. It was hurting her.' She looked past him, up the tangled pathway, wondering if this next stage would go any better than the first. 'Thank you.'

She could hardly hear the mumbled response. 'I did this for my sister. Not for you.'

Tam took her first step along the unknown driveway, not

looking around when he thumped his door closed and took off with a jagged gravel cough. She would find a way. A way to retrieve the beat of her heart, the joy in her life, and that small hand in her hand.

Zilla would help. Her sister, not by blood but by the violent arc of their conjoined, divided lives. Zilla would help.

Again, and always.

I didn't feel invisible when I was with Robbie. He was the one person I didn't have to protect. I felt free; safe from the sharks that lurked in the depths of my psyche. The sex had lasted all night and into the morning — sex and talking and laughing and finding much more in common than I'd expected.

'You'd like Melbourne, I reckon.' Robbie pushed himself up, leaned his head and shoulders on the wall.

My cheek tingled where it had lain on his chest. 'Too cold.' I pulled the sheet up between my legs, covertly using it to pad myself dry.

'Yeah, but they love us wogs. We're in the majority down there.' He spread his fingers, swooped his hand around his head. 'Not like up here. Everyone's so fucking —'.

'Blonde?'

'Yeah.' He reached for his smokes. 'Want one?'

'Nope.'

He read my face. 'Then I don't either.'

'It's okay.'

'What?' He was distracted by a beeping from his jeans, crumpled at the foot of his bed. 'Hang on a tick.' He checked his phone, and answered. Mumbled a few sounds as he walked, fully nude, over to a glass sliding door onto a narrow balcony.

He grunted a few times; displeased but obsequious.

I reached for my phone and saw that sometime during the night, a text had come in from Zaac. My heart thumped as I opened it. It was one word: *Safe.*

I clutched the phone to my solar plexus for a second, then deleted the message and chucked it into my bag.

Robbie hung up his call and stood for moment, staring out at the lamplit *cul-de-sac*, then came over and threw his phone down on the bed. 'That was Hutchens. I have to pick you up.'

'Too late.' I purred at him, then smiled.

He didn't smile back. 'He wants you at Southport Watch House. They've run an initial tox screen — the girl had a suspicious load of diphenhydramine on board.'

I went from giddy to chilled in a heartbeat. A cold hand of fear closed around my throat. I sat up, drawing the sheet with me. 'What?'

'An over-the-counter sedative. Cough medicine.'

'I mean, what has that got to do with me?'

Robbie rested his palms on the bed, leaning over until his forehead met mine. His voice was low and gentle. 'Nothing at all. But Tony Howard has been singing a song in Hutchens's ear. About you.'

Adrenalin blasted through my legs. 'Robbie, don't let them blame me. Don't let them lock me up.' I tried to explain, to rise. My lungs were full of used air, my balance brittle and broken. I swayed a little, my vision filling with dark clouds.

'Hey, it's okay, Zill. I've got you.' Robbie cupped a strong palm softly around my jawline, and held me steady. 'It doesn't matter what's happened. I trust you. I've got your back.'

I looked into his eyes, wondering if I would have to tell him the truth one day. Dreading that he wouldn't understand. I moved his hand away, and for a moment, saw the fear in his eyes that I would push him away completely. But instead, I nodded and leaned in slowly to nestle my head into the curve of his neck.

He sighed with pleasure and stroked my unruly hair, winding a curl gently around his finger.

My shoulders loosed, dropping away from my ears for the first time in a long, long time.

ABOUT THE AUTHOR

Meg Vann trekked over glaciers with her toddler while pregnant, talked herself out of being mugged on the streets of New York, and was detained for no apparent reason at Uzbekistan airport while on a diplomatic visa.

A crime writer, publisher, and scholar, and an abuse survivor, Meg has been making up thriller stories since before she could read and write. She seeks to confound assumptions about women's criminality and victimhood as part of a broader cultural understanding of gendered violence and the menace of intimacy.

Meg established the Maher Fellowship for Women Writers for regional and Indigenous women to access creative writing development. She is an active member of Australian Crime Writers Association and Sisters in Crime, is the former CEO of Queensland Writers Centre, and regularly appears at writers festivals.

Find out more at megvann.com

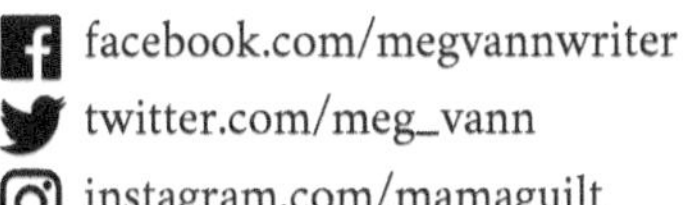

THANK YOU FOR BUYING THIS BRAIN
JAR PRESS CHAPBOOK

To receive special offers, bonus content, and info on
new releases and other great reads,
visit us online at www.BrainJarPress.com

www.ingramcontent.com/pod-product-compliance
Lightning Source LLC
Chambersburg PA
CBHW030846200726

48285CB00007B/2566